THE SHEPHERD

FREDERICK FORSYTH

The Shepherd

ILLUSTRATED BY CHRIS FOSS

HUTCHINSON OF LONDON

Hutchinson & Co (Publishers) Ltd
3 Fitzroy Square, London W1

London Melbourne Sydney Auckland
Wellington Johannesburg and agencies
throughout the world

First published 1975

Set in Monotype Garamond

Printed in Great Britain by The Anchor Press Ltd
and bound by Wm Brendon & Son Ltd
both of Tiptree, Essex

ISBN 0 09 125270 9

The novels of Frederick Forsyth

THE DAY OF THE JACKAL
THE ODESSA FILE
THE DOGS OF WAR

For a brief moment, while waiting for the control tower to clear me for take-off, I glanced out through the perspex cockpit canopy at the surrounding German countryside. It lay white and crisp beneath the crackling December moon.

Behind me lay the boundary fence of the Royal Air Force base, and beyond the fence, as I had seen while swinging my little fighter into line with the take-off runway, the sheet of snow covering the flat farmland stretched away to the line of the pine trees, two miles distant in the night yet so clear I could almost see the shapes of the trees themselves.

Ahead of me as I waited for the voice of the controller to come through the headphones was the runway itself, a slick black ribbon of tarmac, flanked by twin rows of bright-burning lights, illuminating the solid path cut earlier by the snow-ploughs. Behind the lights were the humped banks of the morning's snow, frozen hard once again where the snow-plough blades had pushed them. Far away to my right the airfield tower stood up like a single glowing candle amid the hangars where the muffled aircraftmen were even now closing down the station for the night.

Inside the control tower, I knew, all was warmth

and merriment, the staff waiting only for my departure to close down also, jump into the waiting cars and head back to the parties in the mess. Within minutes of my going, the lights would die out, leaving only the huddled hangars, seeming hunched against the bitter night, the shrouded fighter planes, the sleeping fuel bowser trucks, and above them all the single flickering station light, brilliant red above the black and white airfield, beating out in Morse code the name of the station – CELLE – to an unheeding sky. For tonight there would be no wandering aviators to look down and check their bearings; tonight was Christmas Eve, in the year of grace 1957, and I was a young pilot trying to get home to Blighty for his Christmas leave.

I was in a hurry and my watch said ten-fifteen by the dim blue glow of the control panel where the rows of dials quivered and danced. It was warm and snug inside the cockpit, the heating turned up full to prevent the perspex icing up. It was like a cocoon, small and warm and safe, shielding me from the bitter cold outside, from the freezing night that can kill a man inside a minute if he is exposed to it at 600 miles an hour.

'Charlie Delta . . .'

The controller's voice woke me from my reverie, sounding in my headphones as if he was with me in the tiny cockpit, shouting in my ear. He's had a jar or two already, I thought. Strictly against orders, but what the hell? It's Christmas.

'Charlie Delta . . . Control,' I responded.

'Charlie Delta, clear take-off,' he said.

I saw no point in responding. I simply eased the

throttle forward slowly with the left hand, holding the Vampire steady down the central line with the right hand. Behind me the low whine of the Goblin engine rose and rose, passing through a cry and into a scream. The snub-nosed fighter rolled, the lights each side of the runway passed in ever quicker succession, till they were flashing in a continuous blur. She became light, the nose rose fractionally, freeing the nose-wheel from contact with the runway, and the rumble vanished instantly. Seconds later the main wheels came away and their soft drumming also stopped. I held her low above the deck, letting the speed build up till a glance at the airspeed indicator told me we were through 120 knots and heading for 150. As the end of the runway whizzed beneath my feet I pulled the Vampire into a gently climbing turn to the left, easing up the undercarriage lever as I did so.

From beneath and behind me I heard the dull clunk of the main wheels entering their bays, the lunge forward of the jet as the drag of the undercarriage vanished. In front of me the three red lights representing three wheels extinguished themselves. I held her into the climbing turn, pressing the radio button with the left thumb.

'Charlie Delta, clear airfield, wheels up and locked,' I said into my oxygen mask.

'Charlie Delta, roger, over to Channel D,' said the controller, and then, before I could change radio channels added, 'Happy Christmas.'

Strictly against the rules of radio procedure, of course. I was very young then, and very conscientious. But I replied, 'Thank you, Tower, and same to you.' Then I switched channels to tune in to the RAF's North-Germany Air Control frequency.

Down on my right thigh was strapped the map with my course charted on it in blue ink, but I did not need it. I knew the details by heart, worked out earlier with the Navigation Officer in the Nav. hut. Turn overhead Celle airfield on to course 265 degrees, continue climbing to 27000 feet. On reaching height, maintain course and keep speed to 485 knots. Check in with Channel D to let them know you're in their airspace, then a straight run over the Dutch coast south of Beveland into the North Sea. After forty-four minutes' flying time, change to Channel F and call Lakenheath Control to give you a 'steer'. Fourteen minutes later you'll be overhead Lakenheath. After that, follow instructions, and they'll bring you down on a radio-controlled descent. No problem – all routine procedures. Sixty-six minutes' flying time, with the descent and landing, and the Vampire had enough fuel for over eighty minutes in the air.

Swinging over Celle airfield at 5000 feet, I straightened up and watched the needle on my electric compass settle happily down on a course of 265 degrees. The nose was pointing towards the black freezing vault of the night sky, studded with stars so brilliant they flickered their white fire against the eyeballs. Below, the black-white map of north Germany was growing smaller, the dark masses of the pine forests blending into the white expanses of the fields. Here and there a village or small town glittered with lights. Down there amid the gaily lit streets the carol singers would be out, knocking on the holly-studded doors to sing 'Silent Night' and collect *pfennigs* for charity. The Westphalian house-wives would be preparing hams and geese.

Four hundred miles ahead of me the story would be the same, the carols in my own language but many of the tunes the same, and it would be turkey instead of goose. But whether you call it *Weihnachten* or Christmas, it's the same all over the Christian world, and it was good to be going home.

From Lakenheath I knew I could get a lift down to London in the liberty bus, leaving just after mid-night; from London I was confident I could hitch a lift to my parents' home in Kent. By breakfast time I'd be celebrating with my own family. The alti-meter said 27000 feet. I eased the nose forward, reduced throttle setting to give me an airspeed of 485 knots, and held her steady on 265 degrees. Somewhere beneath me in the gloom the Dutch border would be slipping away, and I had been air-borne for twenty-one minutes. No problem.

The problem started ten minutes out over the North Sea, and it started so quietly that it was several minutes before I realized I had one at all. For some time I had been unaware that the low hum coming through my headphones into my ears had ceased, to be replaced by the strange nothingness of total silence. I must have been failing to concentrate, my thoughts being of home and my waiting family. The first thing I knew was when I flicked a glance down-wards to check my course on the compass. Instead of being rock steady on 265 degrees, the needle was drifting lazily round the clock, passing through east, west, south and north with total impartiality.

I swore a most unseasonal sentiment against the compass and the instrument fitter who should have checked it for 100 per cent reliability. Compass failure at night, even a brilliant moonlit night such as the one beyond the cockpit perspex, was no fun. Still, it was not too serious; I could call up Lakenheath in a few minutes, and they would give me a GCA – Ground Controlled Approach – the second-by-second instructions that a well-equipped airfield can give a pilot to bring him home in the worst of weathers, following his progress on ultra-precise radar screens, watching him descend all the way to the tarmac, tracing his position in the sky yard by yard and second by second. I glanced at my watch: thirty-four minutes airborne. I could try to raise Lakenheath now, at the outside limit of my radio range.

Before trying Lakenheath, it would be correct procedure to inform Channel D, to whom I was tuned, of my little problem, so they could advise Lakenheath I was on my way without a compass. I pressed the 'transmit' button and called.

'Celle Charlie Delta, Celle Charlie Delta, calling North Beveland Control . . .'

I stopped. There was no point in going on. Instead of the lively crackle of static and the sharp sound of my own voice coming back into my own ears, there was a muffled murmur inside my oxygen mask. My own voice speaking . . . and going no-where. I tried again. Same result. Far back across the wastes of the black and bitter North Sea, in the warm cheery concrete complex of North Beveland Control, men sat back from their control panel, chatting and

14

sipping their steaming coffee and cocoa. And they could not hear me. The radio was dead.

Fighting down the rising sense of panic that can kill a pilot faster than anything else, I swallowed and slowly counted to ten. Then I switched to Channel F and tried to raise Lakenheath, ahead of me amid the Suffolk countryside, lying in its forest of pine trees south of Thetford, beautifully equipped with its GCA system for bringing home lost aircraft. On Channel F the radio was as dead as ever. My own muttering into the oxygen mask was smothered by the surrounding rubber. The steady whistle of my own jet engine behind me was my only answer.

It's a very lonely place, the sky, even more so the sky on a winter's night. And a single-seater jet fighter is a lonely home, a tiny steel box held aloft on stubby wings, hurled through the freezing emptiness by a blazing tube throwing out the strength of six thousand horses every second that it burns. But the loneliness is offset, cancelled out, by the knowledge that at the touch of a button on the throttle the pilot can talk to other human beings, people who care about him, men and women who staff a network of stations across the world; just one touch of that button, the 'transmit' button, and scores of them in control towers across the land that are tuned to his channel can hear him call for help. When the pilot transmits, on every one of those screens a line of light streaks from the centre of the screen to the outside rim, which is marked with figures, from One to Three Hundred and Sixty – the number of degrees in a complete compass. Where the streak of light hits the ring, that is where the aircraft lies in relation to the

control tower listening to him. The control towers are linked, so with two cross-bearings they can locate his position to a few hundred yards. He is not lost any more. People begin working to bring him down.

The radar operators pick up the little dot he makes on their screen from all the other dots; they call him up and give him instructions. 'Begin your descent now, Charlie Delta. We have you now. . . .' Warm, experienced voices, voices who control an array of electronic devices that can reach out across the winter sky, through the ice and rain, above the snow and cloud, to pluck the lost one from his deadly infinity and bring him down to the flare-lit runway that means home and life itself.

When the pilot transmits. But for that he must have a radio. Before I had finished testing Channel J, the international emergency channel, and obtained the same negative result, I knew my ten-channel radio set was as dead as the Dodo.

It had taken the RAF two years to train me to fly their fighters for them, and most of that time had been training precisely in emergency procedures. The important thing, they used to say in flying school, is not to know how to fly in perfect conditions; it is to fly through an emergency and stay alive. Now the training was beginning to take effect.

While I was vainly testing my radio channels, the eyes scanned the instrument panel in front of me. The instruments told their own message. It was no coincidence the compass and the radio had failed together; both worked off the aircraft's electrical circuits. Somewhere beneath my feet, amid the miles of brightly coloured wiring that make up the

17

circuits, there had been a main fuse blow-out. I reminded myself, idiotically, to forgive the instrument fitter and blame the electrician. Then I took stock of the nature of my disaster.

The first thing to do in such a case, I remembered old Flight Sergeant Norris telling us, is to reduce throttle setting from cruise speed to a slower setting, to give maximum flight endurance.

'We don't want to waste valuable fuel, do we, gentlemen? We might need it later. So we reduce the power setting from 10000 revolutions per minute to 7200. That way we will fly a little slower, but we will stay in the air rather longer, won't we, gentlemen?' He always referred to us all being in the same emergency at the same time, did Sergeant Norris. I eased the throttle back and watched the rev-counter. But it too was an electrical instrument, and I had lost the lot when the fuse went. I judged by engine note when the Goblin was turning over at about 7200 r.p.m., and felt the aircraft slow down. The nose rose fractionally, so I adjusted the flight-trim to keep her straight and level.

The main instruments in front of a pilot's eyes are six, including the compass. The other five are the airspeed indicator, the altimeter, the bank indicator (which tells him if he's banking, i.e., turning, to left or right), the slip indicator (which tells him if he's skidding crabwise across the sky) and the vertical speed indicator (which tells him if he's diving or climbing and if so how fast). The last three of these are electrically operated, and they had gone the same way as my compass. That left me with the two pressure-operated instruments, airspeed indicator and altimeter. In other words, I knew how fast I was going and how high I was.

It is perfectly possible to land an aircraft with only these two instruments, judging the rest by those old navigational aids, the human eyes. Possible, that is, in conditions of brilliant weather, by daylight and with no cloud in the sky. It is possible, just possible though not advisable, to try and navigate a fast-moving jet by dead-reckoning, using the eyes, looking down and identifying the curve of the coast where it makes an easily recognizable pattern, spotting a strange-shaped reservoir, the glint of a river that the map strapped to the thigh says can only be the Ouse, or the Trent, or the Thames. From lower down it is possible to differentiate Norwich Cathedral tower from Lincoln Cathedral tower, if you know the countryside intimately. By night it is not possible.

The only things that show up at night, even a bright moonlit night, are the lights. These have patterns when seen from the sky. Manchester looks different from Birmingham; Southampton can be recognized from the shape of its massive harbour and the Solent, cut out in black (the sea shows up black) against the carpet of the city's lights. I knew Norwich very well, and if I could identify the great curving bulge of the Norfolk coastline from Lowestoft, round through Yarmouth to Cromer, I could find Norwich, the only major sprawl of lights set twenty miles inland from all points on the coast. Five miles north of Norwich I knew was the fighter airfield of Merriam St George, whose red indicator beacon would be blipping out its Morse identification signal into the night. There, if they only had the sense to switch on the airfield lights when they heard me screaming at low level up and down the airfield, I could land safely.

I began to let the Vampire down slowly towards the oncoming coast, my mind feverishly working out how far behind schedule I was through the reduced speed. My watch told me forty-three minutes airborne. The coast of Norfolk had to be somewhere ahead of my nose, six miles below. I glanced up at the full moon, like a searchlight in the glittering sky, and thanked her for her presence.

As the fighter slipped towards Norfolk the sense of loneliness gripped me tighter and tighter. All those things that had seemed so beautiful as I had climbed away from the Westphalian airfield now seemed my worst enemies. The stars were no longer impressive in their brilliance; I thought of their hostility, sparkling away there in the timeless, lost infinities, of endless sub-zero space. The night sky, its stratospheric temperature fixed, night and day alike, at an unchanging fifty-six degrees below zero, became in my mind a limitless prison creaking with the cold. Below me lay the worst of them all, the heavy brutality of the North Sea, waiting to swallow up me and my plane and bury us for endless eternity in a liquid crypt where nothing moved, nor would ever move again. And no one would ever know.

At 15 000 feet and still diving, I began to realize that a fresh, and for me the last, enemy had entered the field. There was no ink-black sea three miles below me, no necklace of twinkling seaside lights somewhere up ahead. Far away, to right and left, ahead and no doubt behind me, the light of the moon reflected on a flat and endless sea of white. Perhaps only a hundred, two hundred, feet thick, but enough. Enough to blot out all vision, enough to kill me. The East Anglian fog had moved in.

As I had flown westwards from Germany a slight breeze, unforeseen by the weather men, had sprung up blowing from the North Sea towards Norfolk. During the previous day the flat, open ground of East Anglia had been frozen hard by the wind and the sub-zero temperatures. During the evening the wind had moved a belt of slightly warmer air off the North Sea and on to the plains of East Anglia. There, coming in contact with the ice-cold earth, the trillions of tiny moisture particles in the sea air had vapourized, forming the kind of fog that can blot out five counties in a matter of thirty minutes. How far westward it stretched I could not tell; to the West Midlands, perhaps, nudging up against the eastern slopes of the Pennines? There was no question of trying to overfly the fog to the west-wards; without navigational aids or radio, I would be lost over strange, unfamiliar country. Also out of the question was to try and fly back to Holland, to land at one of the Dutch air force bases along the coast there; I had not the fuel. Relying only on my eyes to guide me, it was a question of landing at Merriam St George or dying amid the wreckage of the Vampire somewhere in the fog-wreathed fens of Norfolk.

At 10000 feet I pulled out of my dive, increasing power slightly to keep myself airborne, using up more of my precious fuel. Still a creature of my training, I recalled the instructions of Flight Sergeant Norris again.

'When we are totally lost above unbroken cloud, gentlemen, we must consider the necessity of baling out of our aircraft, must we not?'

Of course, Sergeant. Unfortunately the Martin Baker ejector seat cannot be fitted to the single seat Vampire which is notorious for being almost impossible to bale out of, the only two successful candidates living lost their legs in the process. Still, there has to be a first lucky one. What else, Sergeant?

'Our first move, therefore, is to turn our aircraft towards the open sea, away from all areas of intense human habitation.'

You mean towns, Sergeant. These people down there pay for us to fly for them, not to drop a screaming monster of ten tons of steel on top of them on Christmas Eve. There are kids down there, schools, hospitals, homes. You turn your aircraft out to sea.

The procedures were all worked out. They did not mention that the chances of a pilot, bobbing about in a winter's night in the North Sea, frozen face lashed by sub-zero wind, supported by a yellow life-jacket, ice encrusting on his lips, eyebrows, ears, his position unknown by the men sipping their Christmas punches in warm rooms three hundred miles away – that his chances were less than one in a hundred of living longer than one hour. In the training films they showed you pictures of happy fellows who had announced by radio that they were ditching, being picked up by helicopters within minutes, and all on a bright, warm summer's day.

'One last procedure, gentlemen, to be used in extreme emergency.'

That's better, Sergeant Norris, that's what I'm in now.

'All haircraft happroaching Britain's coasts are visible on the radar scanners of our early warning system. If, therefore, we have lost our radio, and cannot transmit our emergency, we try to attract the attention of our radar scanners by adopting an odd form of behaviour. We do this by moving out to sea, then flying in small triangles, turning left, left, and left again, each leg of the triangle being of a duration of two minutes' flying time. In this way we hope to attract attention. When we have been spotted, the air traffic controller is informed, and he diverts another aircraft to find us. This other aircraft of course has radio. When discovered by the rescue aircraft, we formate on him, and he brings us down through the cloud or fog to a safe landing.'

Yes, it was the last attempt to save one's life. I recalled the details better now. The rescue aircraft who would lead you back to a safe landing, flying wing-tip to wing-tip, was called the shepherd. I glanced at my watch; fifty-one minutes airborne, thirty minutes left of fuel. The fuel gauge read one-third full. Knowing myself to be still short of the Norfolk coast, and flying level at 10000 feet in the moonlight, I pulled the Vampire into a left-hand turn and began my first leg of the first triangle. After two minutes, I pulled left again, hoping (without a compass) to be able to judge 120 degrees, using the moon as a rough guide. Below me the fog reached back as far as I could see, and ahead of me also, towards Norfolk, it was the same.

Ten minutes went by, nearly two complete triangles. I had not prayed, not really prayed, for many years and the habit came hard. Lord, please get me out of this bloody mess . . . no, you mustn't talk like that to Him. Our Father, which art in Heaven . . . he'd heard that a thousand times, would be hearing it another thousand times tonight. What do you say to Him when you want help? Please, God, make somebody notice me up here, please make someone see me flying in triangles and send up a shepherd to help me down to a safe landing. Please help me, and I promise . . . What on earth could I promise Him? He had no need of me, and I who now had need of Him had taken no notice of Him for so long He'd probably forgotten all about me.

By seventy-two minutes airborne on my watch I knew no one would come. The compass still drifted aimlessly through all the points of the circle, the other electrical instruments were dead, all their needles pointing at zero. My altimeter said 7000 feet, so I had dropped 3000 feet while turning. No matter. The fuel read almost one-eighth full – say ten minutes' more flying time. I felt the rage of despair welling up. I began screaming into the dead microphone.

You stupid bastards, why don't you look at your radar screens? Why can't somebody see me up here? All so damn drunk you can't do your jobs properly. Oh God, why won't somebody listen to me? By then the anger had subsided and I had taken to blubbering like a baby from the sheer helplessness of it all.

Five minutes later I knew, without any doubt of it, that I was going to die that night. Strangely, I wasn't even afraid any more. Just enormously sad. Sad for all the things I would never do, the places I would never see, the people I would never greet again. It's a bad thing, a sad thing, to die at twenty years old with your life unlived, and the worst thing of all is not the fact of dying but the fact of all the things never done.

Out through the perspex I could see the moon was setting, hovering above the horizon of thick white fog; in another two minutes the night sky would be plunged into total darkness and a few minutes later I would have to bale out of a dying aircraft before it flicked over on its last dive into the North Sea. An hour later I would be dead also, bobbing around in the water, a bright yellow Mae West jacket supporting a stiff, frozen body. I dropped the left wing of the Vampire towards the moon to bring the aircraft on to the final leg of the last triangle.

Down below the wing-tip, against the sheen of the fog bank, up moon of me, a black shadow crossed the whiteness. For a second I thought it was my own shadow, but with the moon up there my own shadow would be behind me. It was another aircraft, low against the fog bank, keeping station with me through my turn, a mile down through the sky towards the fog.

The other aircraft being below me, I kept turning, wing down, to keep it in sight. The other aircraft also kept turning, until the two of us had done one complete circle. Only then did I realize why it was so far below me, why he did not climb to my height and take up station on my wing-tip. He was flying slower than I, he could not keep up if he tried to fly beside me. Trying hard not to believe he was just another aircraft, moving on his way, about to disappear for ever into the fog bank, I eased the throttle back and began to slip down towards him. He kept turning; so did I. At 5000 feet I knew I was still going too fast for him. I could not reduce power any more for fear of stalling the Vampire and plunging down out of control. To slow up even more I put out the air brakes. The Vampire shuddered as the brakes swung into the slipstream, slowing the Vampire down to 280 knots.

And then he came up towards me, swinging in towards my left-hand wing-tip. I could make out the black bulk of him against the dim white sheet of fog below, then he was with me, a hundred feet off my wing-tip, and we straightened out together, rocking as we tried to keep formation. The moon was to my right, and my own shadow masked his shape and form, but even so I could make out the shimmer of two propellers whirling through the sky ahead of him. Of course he could not fly at my speed; I was in a jet fighter, he in a piston-engined aircraft of an earlier generation.

He held station alongside me for a few seconds, down moon of me, half invisible, then banked gently to the left. I followed, keeping formation with him, for he was obviously the shepherd sent up to bring me down, and he had the compass and the radio, not I. He swung through 180 degrees then straightened up, flying straight and level, the moon behind him. From the position of the dying moon I knew we were heading back towards the Norfolk coast, and for the first time I could see him well. To my surprise, my shepherd was a De Havilland Mosquito, a fighter-bomber of Second World War vintage.

Then I remembered that the Meteorological Squadron at Gloucester used Mosquitoes, the last ones flying, to take samples of the upper atmosphere to help in the preparation of weather forecasts. I had seen them at Battle of Britain displays, flying their Mosquitoes in the fly-pasts, attracting gasps from the crowd and a few nostalgic shakes of the head from the older men, such as they always reserved on September 15th for the Spitfires, Hurricanes and Lancasters.

Inside the cockpit of the Mosquito I could make out, against the light of the moon, the muffled head of its pilot and the twin circles of his goggles as he looked out of the side window towards me. Carefully he raised his right hand till I could see it in the window, fingers straight, palm downwards. He jabbed the fingers forward and down, meaning, 'We are going to descend, formate on me.'

I nodded and quickly brought up my own left hand so he could see it, pointing forwards to my own control panel with one forefinger, then holding up my five splayed fingers. Finally I drew my hand across my throat. By common agreement this sign means I have only five minutes' fuel left, then my engine cuts out. I saw the muffled, goggled, oxygen-masked head nod in understanding, then we were heading downwards towards the sheet of fog. His speed increased and I brought the airbrakes back in.

The Vampire stopped trembling and plunged ahead of the Mosquito. I pulled back on the throttle, hearing the engine die to a low whistle, and the shepherd was back beside me. We were diving straight towards the shrouded land of Norfolk. I glanced at my altimeter: 2000 feet, still diving.

He pulled out at three hundred feet, the fog was still below us. Probably the fog bank was only from the ground to 100 feet up, but that was more than enough to prevent a plane from landing without a GCA. I could imagine the stream of instructions coming from the radar hut into the earphones of the man flying beside me, eighty feet away through two panes of perspex and a windstream of icy air moving between us at 280 knots. I kept my eyes on him, formating as closely as possible, afraid of losing sight for an instant, watching for his every hand-signal. Against the white fog, even as the moon sank, I had to marvel at the beauty of his aircraft; the short nose and bubble cockpit, the blister of perspex right in the nose itself with the twin cannon pointing out towards the enemy, the long, lean, underslung engine pods, each housing a Rolls-Royce Merlin engine, a masterpiece of craftsmanship, snarling through the night towards home. Two minutes later he held up his clenched left fist in the window, then opened the fist to splay all five fingers against the glass. Please lower your undercarriage. I moved the lever downwards and felt the dull thunk as all three wheels went down, happily powered by hydraulic pressure and not dependent on the failed electrical system.

The pilot of the shepherd aircraft pointed down

again, for another descent, and as he jinked in the moonlight I caught sight of the nose of the Mosquito. It had the letters JK painted on it, large and black. Probably for call-sign Juliet Kilo. Then we were descending again, more gently this time.

He levelled out just above the fog layer, so low the tendrils of candy-floss were lashing at our fuselages, and we went into a steady circular turn. I managed to flick a glance at my fuel gauge: it was on zero, flickering feebly. For God's sake, hurry up, I prayed, for if my fuel failed me now there would be no time to climb to the minimum 500 feet needed for bailing out. A jet fighter at 100 feet without an engine is a death-trap with no chances for survival.

For two or three minutes he seemed content to hold his slow circular turn, while, the sweat broke out behind my neck and began to run in streams down my back, gumming the light nylon flying suit to my skin. HURRY UP, MAN, HURRY.

Quite suddenly he straightened out, so fast I almost lost him by continuing to turn. I caught him a second later and saw his left hand flash the 'dive' signal to me. Then he dipped towards the fog bank, I followed, and we were in it, a shallow, flat descent, but a descent nevertheless, and from a mere hundred feet, towards nothing.

To pass out of even dimly lit sky into cloud or fog is like passing into a bath of grey cotton wool. Suddenly there is nothing but the grey whirling strands, a million tendrils reaching out to trap and strangle you, each one touching the cockpit cover with quick caress then disappearing back into nothingness. The visibility was down to near zero, no shape, no size, no form, no substance. Except that dimly off my left wing-tip, now only forty feet away, was the form of a Mosquito flying with absolute certainty towards something I could not see. Only then did I realize he was flying without lights. For a second I was amazed, horrified by my discovery; then I realized the widsom of the man. Lights in fog are treacherous, hallucinatory, mesmeric. You can get attracted to them, not knowing whether they are forty or a hundred feet away from you. The tendency is to move towards them; for two aircraft in the fog, one flying formation on the other, that could spell disaster. The man was right.

Keeping formation with him, I knew he was slowing down, for I too was easing back the throttle, dropping and slowing. In a fraction of a second I flashed a glance at the two instruments I needed: the altimeter was reading zero, so was the fuel gauge, and neither was even flickering. The airspeed indicator, which I had also seen, read 120 knots – and this damn coffin was going to fall out of the sky at 95.

Without warning the shepherd pointed a single forefinger at me, then forward through the windscreen. It meant 'There you are, fly on and land.' I stared forward through the now streaming windscreen. Nothing. Then, yes, something. A blur to the left, another to the right, then two, one each side. Ringed with haze, there were lights either side of me, in pairs, flashing past. I forced my eyes to see what lay between them. Nothing, blackness. Then a streak of paint, running under my feet. The centre line. Frantically I closed down the power and held her steady, praying for the Vampire to settle.

The lights were rising now, almost at eye level, and still she would not settle. Bang. We touched, we touched the deck. Bang-bang. Another touch, she was drifting again, inches above the wet black runway. Bam-bam-bam-babam-rumble. She was down. The main wheels had stuck and held.

The Vampire was rolling, at over ninety miles an hour, through a sea of grey fog. I touched the brakes and the nose slammed down on to the deck also. Slow pressure now, no skidding, hold her straight against the skid, more pressure on those brakes or we'll run off the end. The lights moving past more leisurely now, slowing, slower, slower. . . .

The Vampire stopped. I found both my hands clenched round the control column, squeezing the brake lever inwards. I forget now how many seconds I held them there before I would believe we were stopped. Finally I did believe it, put on the parking brake and released the main brake. Then I went to turn off the engine, for there was no use trying to taxi in this fog; they would have to tow the fighter back with a Land-Rover. There was no need to turn off the engine; it had finally run out of fuel as the Vampire careered down the runway. I shut off the remaining systems, fuel, hydraulics, electrics and pressurization, and slowly began to unstrap myself from the seat and parachute/dinghy pack. As I did so a movement caught my eye. To my left, through the fog, no more than fifty feet away, low on the ground with wheels up, the Mosquito roared past me. I caught the flash of the pilot's hand in the side window, then he was gone, up into the fog before he could see my answering wave of acknowledgement. But I'd already decided to call up RAF Gloucester and thank him personally from the officers' mess.

With the systems off, the cockpit was misting up fast, so I released the canopy and pushed it upwards and backwards by hand until it locked. Only then, as I stood up, did I realize how cold it was. Against my heated body, dressed in light nylon flying suit, it was freezing. I expected the control-tower truck to be alongside in seconds, for with an emergency landing, even on Christmas Eve, the fire truck, ambulance and half a dozen other vehicles were always standing by. Nothing happened. At least, not for ten minutes.

By the time the two headlights came groping out of the mist I felt frozen. The lights stopped twenty feet from the motionless Vampire, dwarfed by the fighter's bulk. A voice called:

'Hallo there.'

I stepped out of the cockpit, jumped from the wing to the ground and ran towards the lights. They turned out to be the headlamps of a battered old Jowett Javelin. Not an Air Force identification mark in sight. At the wheel of the car was a puffed, beery face and a handlebar moustache. At least he wore an RAF officer's cap. He stared at me as I loomed out of the fog.

'That yours?' He nodded towards the dim shape of the Vampire.

'Yes,' I said, 'I just landed it.'

'Straordinary,' he said, 'quite straordinary. You'd

better jump in. I'll run you back to the mess.'

I was grateful for the warmth of the car, even more so to be alive.

Moving in bottom gear he began to ease the old car back round the taxi-track, evidently towards the control tower and beyond them the mess buildings. As we moved away from the Vampire I saw that I had stopped twenty feet short of a ploughed field at the very end of the runway.

'You were damned lucky,' he said, or rather shouted, for the engine was roaring in first gear and he seemed to be having trouble with the foot controls. Judging by the smell of whisky on his breath, that was not surpising.

'Damned lucky,' I agreed. 'I ran out of fuel just as I was landing. My radio and all the electrical systems failed nearly fifty minutes ago over the North Sea.'

He spent several minutes digesting the information carefully.

'Straordinary,' he said at length. 'No compass?'

'No compass. Flying in the approximate direction by the moon. As far as the coast, or where I judged it to be. After that . . .'

'No radio?'

'No radio,' I said. 'A dead box on all channels.'

'Then how did you find this place?' he asked.

I was losing patience. The man was evidently one of those passed-over flight lieutenants, not terribly bright and probably not a flyer, despite the handle-bar moustache. A ground wallah. And drunk with it. Shouldn't be on duty at all on an operational station at that hour of the night.

36

'I was guided in,' I explained patiently. The emergency procedures, having worked so well, now began to seem run-o'-the-mill, such is the recuperation of youth. 'I flew short, left-hand triangles, as per instructions, and they sent up a shepherd aircraft to guide me down. No problem.'

He shrugged, as if to say 'if you insist'. Finally he said:

'Damn lucky, all the same. I'm surprised the other chap managed to find the place.'

'No problem there,' I explained patiently. 'It was one of the weather aircraft from RAF Gloucester. Obviously he had radio. So we came in here in formation, on a GCA. Then when I saw the lights at the threshold of the runway, I landed myself.'

The man was obviously dense, as well as drunk.

'Straordinary,' he said, sucking a stray drop of moisture off his handlebar. 'We don't have GCA. We don't have any navigational equipment at all, not even a beacon.'

Now it was my turn to let the information sink in.

'This isn't RAF Merriam St George?' I asked in a small voice. He shook his head. 'Marham? Chicksands? Lakenheath?'

'No,' he said, 'this is RAF Minton.'

'I've never heard of it,' I said at last.

'I'm not surprised. We're not an operational station. Haven't been for years. Minton's a storage depot. Excuse me.'

He stopped the car and got out. I saw we were standing a few feet from the dim shape of a control tower, adjoining a long row of Nissen huts, evidently once flight rooms, navigational and briefing huts.

37

Above the narrow door at the base of the tower through which the officer had disappeared hung a single naked bulb. By its light I could make out broken windows, padlocked doors, an air of abandonment and neglect. The man returned and climbed shakily back behind the wheel.

'Just turning the runway lights off,' he said, and belched.

My mind was whirling. This was mad, crazy, illogical. Yet there had to be a perfectly reasonable explanation.

'Why did you switch them on?' I asked.

'It was the sound of your engine,' he said. 'I was in the officers' mess having a noggin, and old Joe suggested I listen out the window for a second. There you were, circling right above us. You sounded damn low, almost as if you were going to come down in a hurry. Thought I might be of some use, remembered they never disconnected the old runway lights when they dismantled the station, so I ran down to the control tower and switched them on.'

'I see,' I said, but I didn't. But there had to be an explanation.

'That was why I was so late coming out to pick you up. I had to go back to the mess to get the car out, once I'd heard you land out there. Then I had to find you. Bloody foggy night.'

You can say that again, I thought. The mystery puzzled me for another few minutes. Then I hit on the explanation.

'Where is RAF Minton, exactly?' I asked him.

'Five miles in from the coast, inland from Cromer.

That's where we are,' he said.

'And where's the nearest operational RAF station with all the radio aids including GCA?'

He thought for a minute.

'Must be Merriam St George,' he said. 'They must have all those things. Mind you, I'm just a stores johnny.'

That was the explanation. My unknown friend in the weather plane had been taking me straight from the coast for Merriam St George. By chance Minton, abandoned old stores depot Minton, with its cobwebbed runway lights and drunken commanding officer, lay right along the in-flight path to Merriam's runway. Merriam controller had asked us to circle twice while he switched on his runway lights ten miles ahead, and this old fool had switched on his lights as well. Result: coming in on the last ten-mile stretch, I had plonked my Vampire down on the wrong airfield. I was about to tell him not to interfere with modern procedures that he couldn't understand when I choked the words back. My fuel had run out halfway down the runway. I'd never have made Merriam, ten miles away. I'd have crashed in the fields short of touchdown. By an amazing fluke I had been, as he said, damned lucky.

By the time I had worked out the rational explanation for my presence at this nearly abandoned airfield, we had reached the officers' mess. My host parked his car in front of the door and we climbed out. Above the entrance hall a light was burning, dispelling the fog and illuminating the carved but chipped crest of the Royal Air Force above the doorway. To one side was a board screwed to the wall. It said 'RAF Station Minton'. To the other side was another board announcing 'Officers' Mess'. We walked inside.

The front hall was large and spacious, but evidently built in the pre-war years when metal window-frames, service issue, were in the fashion. The place reeked of the expression 'it had seen better days'. It had indeed. Only two cracked leather club chairs occupied the ante room, which could have taken twenty. The cloakroom to the right contained a long empty rail for non-existent coats. My host, who told me he was Flight Lieutenant Marks, shrugged off his sheepskin coat and threw it over a chair. He was wearing his uniform trousers, but with a chunky blue pullover for a jacket. It must be miserable to spend your Christmas on duty in a dump like this.

He told me he was the second-in-command, the CO being a squadron leader now on Christmas leave. Apart from him and his CO, the station boasted a sergeant, three corporals, one of whom was on Christmas duty and presumably in the corporals' mess also on his own, and twenty stores clerks, all away on leave. When not on leave, they spent their days classifying tons of surplus clothing, parachutes, boots, and other impedimenta that goes to make up a fighting service.

There was no fire in the vestibule, though there was a large brick fireplace, nor any in the bar either. Both rooms were freezing cold, and I was beginning to shiver again after recovering in the car. Marks was putting his head through the various doors leading off the hall, shouting for someone called Joe. By looking through after him, I took in at a glance the spacious but deserted dining room, also fireless and cold, and the twin passages, one leading to the officers' private rooms, the other to the staff quarters. RAF messes do not vary much in architecture; once a pattern, always a pattern.

'I'm sorry it's not very hospitable, old boy,' said Marks, having failed to find the absent Joe. 'Being only the two of us on station here, and no visitors to speak of, we've each made two bedrooms into a sort of self-contained apartment where we live. Hardly seems worth using all this space just for the two of us. You can't heat them in winter, you know; not on the fuel they allow us. And you can't get the stuff.'

It seemed sensible. In his position I'd probably have done the same.

'Not to worry,' I said, dropping my flying helmet and attached oxygen mask into the other leather chair. 'Though I could do with a bath and a meal.'

'I think we can manage that,' he said, trying hard to play the genial host. 'I'll get Joe to fix up one of the spare rooms – God knows we have enough of them – and heat up the water. He'll also rustle up a meal. Not much, I'm afraid. Bacon and eggs do?'

I nodded. By this time I presumed old Joe was the mess steward.

'That will do fine. While I'm waiting, do you mind if I use your phone?'

'Certainly, certainly, of course, you'll have to check in.'

He ushered me into the mess secretary's office, a door beside the entrance to the bar. It was small and cold, but it had a chair, empty desk and a telephone.

I dialled 100 for the local operator and while I was waiting Marks returned with a tumbler of whisky. Normally I hardly touched spirits, but it was warming, so I thanked him and he went off to supervise the steward. My watch told me it was close to midnight. Hell of a way to spend Christmas, I thought. Then I recalled how thirty minutes earlier I had been crying to God for a bit of help, and felt ashamed.

'Little Minton,' said a drowsy voice. It took ages to get through, for I had no telephone number for Merriam St George, but the girl got it eventually. Down the line I could hear the telephone operator's family celebrating in a back room, no doubt the living quarters attached to the village post office. Eventually the phone was ringing.

'RAF Merriam St George,' said a man's voice. Duty sergeant speaking from the guard-room, I thought.

'Duty Controller, Air Traffic Control, please,' I said. There was a pause.

'I'm sorry, sir,' said the voice, 'may I ask who's calling?'

I gave him my name and rank. Speaking from RAF Minton, I told him.

'I see, sir. But I'm afraid there's no flying tonight, sir. No one on duty in Air Traffic Control. A few of the officers up in the mess though.'

'Then give me the station duty officer, please.'

When I got through to him he was evidently in the mess, for the sound of lively talk could be heard behind him. I explained about the emergency and the fact that his station had been alerted to receive a Vampire fighter coming in on an emergency GCA without radio. He listened attentively. Perhaps he was young and conscientious too, for he was quite sober, as a station duty officer is supposed to be at all times, even Christmas.

'I don't know about that,' he said at length. 'I don't think we've been operational since we closed down at five this afternoon. But I'm not on Air Traffic. Would you hold on. I'll get the Wing Commander (Flying). He's here.'

There was a pause and then an older voice came on the line. I explained the matter again.

'Where are you speaking from?' he said after noting my name, rank and the station I was based at.

'RAF Minton, sir. I've just made an emergency landing here. Apparently it's nearly abandoned.'

'Yes, I know,' he drawled. 'Damn bad luck. Do you want us to send a Tilly for you?'

'No, it's not that, sir. I don't mind being here. It's just that I landed at the wrong airfield. I believe I was heading for your airfield on a Ground Controlled Approach.'

'Well, make up your mind. Were you or weren't you? You ought to know. According to what you say, you were flying the damn thing.'

I took a deep breath and started at the beginning.

'So you see, sir, I was intercepted by the weather plane from Gloucester, and he brought me in. But in this fog it must have been on a GCA. No other way to get down. Yet when I saw the lights of Minton I landed here assuming it to be Merriam St George.'

'Splendid,' he said at length. 'Marvellous bit of flying by that pilot from Gloucester. 'Course, those chaps are up in all weathers. It's their job. What do you want us to do about it?'

I was getting exasperated. Wing commander he might have been, but he had had a skinful this Christmas Eve.

'I am ringing to alert you to stand down your radar and traffic control crews, sir. They must be waiting for a Vampire that's never going to arrive. It's already arrived – here at Minton.'

'But we're closed down,' he said. 'We shut all the systems down at five o'clock. There's been no call for us to turn out.'

'But Merriam St George has a GCA,' I protested.

'I know we have,' he shouted back. 'But it hasn't been used tonight. It's been shut down since five o'clock.'

I asked the next and last question slowly and carefully.

'Do you know, sir, where is the nearest RAF station that will be manning 121·5 metre band throughout the night, the nearest station to here that maintains twenty-four-hour emergency listening?'

(121·5 metres is the international aircraft emergency frequency.)

'Yes,' he said equally slowly. 'To the west, RAF Marham. To the south, RAF Lakenheath. Good night to you. Happy Christmas.'

He put the phone down. I sat back and breathed deeply. Marham was forty miles away on the other side of Norfolk. Lakenheath was forty miles to the south, in Suffolk. On the fuel I was carrying, not only could I not have made Merriam St George, it wasn't even open. So how could I ever have got to Marham or Lakenheath? And I had told that Mosquito pilot that I only had five minutes' fuel left. He had acknowledged that he understood. In any case, he was flying far too low after we dived into the fog ever to fly forty miles like that. The man must have been mad.

It began to dawn on me that I didn't really owe my life to the weather pilot from Gloucester, but to Flight Lieutenant Marks, beery, bumbling old passed-over Flight Lieutenant Marks, who couldn't tell one end of an aircraft from another but who had run four hundred yards through the fog to switch on the lights of an abandoned runway because he heard a jet engine circling overhead too close to the ground. Still, the Mosquito must be back at Gloucester by now, and he ought to know that despite everything I was alive.

'Gloucester?' said the operator. 'At this time of night?'

'Yes,' I replied firmly, 'Gloucester, at this time of night.'

One thing about weather squadrons, they're always on duty. The duty meteorologist took the call. I explained the position to him.

'I'm afraid there must be some mistake, Flying Officer,' he said. 'It could not have been one of ours.'

'Look, that *is* RAF Gloucester, right?'

'Yes, it is. Duty Met. Officer speaking.'

'Fine. And your unit flies Mosquitoes to take pressure and temperature readings at altitude, right?'

'Wrong,' he said. 'We used to use Mosquitoes.

They went out of service three months ago. We now use Canberras.'

I sat holding the telephone, staring at it in disbelief. Then an idea came to me.

'What happened to them?' I asked. He must have been an elderly boffin of great courtesy and patience to tolerate darn fool questions at this hour of the night.

'They were scrapped, I think, or sent off to museums, more likely. They're getting quite rare nowadays, you know.'

'I know,' I said. 'Could one of them have been sold privately?'

'I suppose it's possible,' he said at length. 'It would depend on Air Ministry policy. But I think they went to aircraft museums.'

'Thank you. Thank you very much. And Happy Christmas.'

I put the phone down and shook my head in bewilderment. What a night, what an incredible night. First I lose my radio and all my instruments, then I get lost and short of fuel, then I am taken in tow by some moonlighting harebrain with a passion for veteran aircraft flying his own Mosquito through the night, who happens to spot me, comes within an inch of killing me and finally a half-drunk ground-duty officer has the sense to put his runway lights on in time to save me. Luck doesn't come in much bigger slices. But one thing was certain: that amateur air ace hadn't the faintest idea what he was doing. On the other hand, where would I be without him, I asked. Bobbing around dead in the North Sea by now.

I raised the last of the whisky to him and his strange passion for flying privately in out-dated aircraft and tossed the drink back. Flight Lieutenant Marks put his head round the door.

'Your room's ready,' he said. 'Number Seventeen, just down the corridor. Joe's making up a fire for you now. The bath water's heating. If you don't mind, I think I'll turn in. Will you be all right on your own?'

I greeted him with more friendliness than last time, which he deserved.

'Sure, I'll be fine. Many thanks for all your help.'

I took my helmet and wandered down the corridor, flanked with the numbers of the bedrooms of bachelor officers long since posted elsewhere. From the door of Seventeen a bar of light shone out into the passage. As I entered the room an old man rose from his knees in front of the fireplace. He gave me a start. Mess stewards are usually RAF serving men. This one was near seventy and obviously a locally recruited civilian employee.

'Good evening, sir,' he said. 'I'm Joe, sir. I'm the mess steward.'

'Yes, Joe, Mr Marks told me about you. Sorry to cause you so much trouble at this hour of the night. I just dropped in, as you might say.'

'Yes, Mr Marks told me. I'll have your room ready directly. Soon as this fire burns up, it'll be quite cosy.'

The chill had not been taken off the room, and I shivered in the nylon flying suit. I should have asked Marks for the loan of a sweater, but had forgotten.

I elected to take my lonely evening meal in my room, and while Joe went to fetch it I had a quick bath, for the water was by now reasonably hot. While I towelled myself down and wrapped the old but warm dressing gown that old Joe had brought with him round me, he set out a small table and placed a plate of sizzling bacon and eggs on it. By now the room was comfortably warm, the coal fire burning brightly, the curtains drawn. While I ate, which took only a few minutes, for I was ravenously hungry, the old steward stayed to talk.

'You been here long, Joe?' I asked him, more out of politeness than genuine interest.

'Oh, yes, sir, nigh on twenty years; since just before the war when the station opened.'

'You've seen some changes, eh? Wasn't always like this.'

'That it wasn't, sir, that it wasn't.' And he told me of the days when the rooms were crammed with eager young pilots, the dining room noisy with the clatter of plates and cutlery, the bar roaring with bawdy songs; of months and years when the sky above the airfield crackled and snarled to the sound of piston engines driving planes to war and bringing them back again.

While he talked I finished my meal and emptied the remainder of the half-bottle of red wine he had brought from the bar store. A very good steward was Joe. After finishing I rose from the table, fished a cigarette from the pocket of my flying suit, lit it and sauntered round the room. The steward began to tidy up the plates and the glass from the table. I halted before an old photograph in a frame, stand-

48

ing alone on the mantelshelf above the crackling fire. I stopped with my cigarette half raised to my lips, feeling the room go suddenly cold.

The photo was old and stained, but behind its glass it was still clear enough. It showed a young man of about my own years, in his early twenties, dressed in flying gear. But not the blue nylon suits and gleaming plastic crash helmet of today. He wore thick sheepskin-lined boots, rough serge trousers and the heavy sheepskin zip-up jacket. From his left hand dangled one of the soft-leather flying helmets they used to wear, with goggles attached, instead of the modern pilot's tinted visor. He stood with legs apart, right hand on hip, a defiant stance, but he was not smiling. He stared at the camera with grim intentness. There was something sad about the eyes.

Behind him, quite clearly visible, stood his aircraft. There was no mistaking the lean, sleek silhouette of the Mosquito fighter-bomber, nor the two low-slung pods housing the twin Merlin engines that gave it its remarkable performance. I was about to say something to Joe when I felt the gust of cold air on my back. One of the windows had blown open and the icy air was rushing in.

'I'll close it, sir,' the old man said, and made to put all the plates back down again.

'No, I'll do it.'

It took me two strides to cross to where the window swung on its steel frame. To get a better hold I stepped inside the curtain and stared out. The fog swirled in waves around the old mess building, disturbed by the current of warm air coming from the window. Somewhere, far away in the fog, I

thought I heard the snarl of engines. There were no engines out there, just a motor cycle of some farm boy, taking leave of his sweetheart across the fens. I closed the window, made sure it was secure, and turned back into the room.

'Who's the pilot, Joe?'

'The pilot, sir?'

I nodded towards the lonely photograph on the mantelshelf.

'Oh, I see, sir. That's a photo of Mr Kavanagh. He was here during the war, sir.'

He placed the wineglass on top of the topmost plate in his hands.

'Kavanagh?' I walked back to the picture and studied it closely.

'Yes, sir. An Irish gentleman. A very fine man, if I may say so. As a matter of fact, sir, this was his room.'

'What squadron was that, Joe?' I was still peering at the aircraft in the background.

'Pathfinders, sir. Mosquitoes, they flew. Remarkable pilots, all of them, sir. But I venture to say I believe Mister Johnny was the best of them all. But then I'm biased, sir. I was his batman, you see.'

There was no doubting it. The faint letters on the nose of the Mosquito behind the figure in the photo read JK. Not Juliet Kilo, but Johnny Kavanagh.

The whole thing was clear as day. Kavanagh had been a superb pilot, flying with one of the crack squadrons during the war. After the war he'd left the Air Force, probably going into second-hand car dealing, as quite a few did. So he'd made a pile of money in the booming fifties, probably bought himself a smart country house, and had enough left over to indulge his real passion – flying. Or rather re-creating the past, his days of glory. He'd bought up an old Mosquito in one of the RAF periodic auctions of obsolescent aircraft, re-fitted it, and flew it privately whenever he wished. Not a bad way to spend your spare time, if you had the money.

So he'd been flying back from some trip to Europe, had spotted me turning in triangles above the cloud bank, realized I was stuck, and taken me in tow. Pin-pointing his position precisely by crossed radio beacons, knowing this stretch of the coast by heart, he'd taken a chance of finding his old airfield at Minton even in thick fog. It was a hell of a risk. But then I had no fuel left anyway, so it was that or bust.

I had no doubt I could trace the man, probably through the Royal Aero club.

'He was certainly a good pilot,' I said reflectively, thinking of this evening's performance.

'The best, sir,' said old Joe from behind me. 'They reckoned he had eyes like a cat, did Mister Johnny. I remember many's the time the squadron would return from dropping flares over bombing targets in Germany, and the rest of the young gentlemen would go into the bar and have a drink. More likely several.'

'He didn't drink?' I asked.

'Oh yes, sir, but more often he'd have his Mosquito re-fuelled and take off again alone, going back over the Channel or the North Sea to see if he could find some crippled bomber making for the coast and guide them home.'

I frowned. These big bombers had their own bases to go to.

'But some of them would have taken a lot of enemy flak fire, and sometimes they had their radios knocked out. All over, they came from. Marham, Scampton, Cotteshall, Waddington; the big four-engined ones, Halifaxes, Stirlings and Lancasters; a bit before your time if you'll pardon my saying so, sir.'

'I've seen pictures of them,' I admitted. 'And some of them fly in air parades. And he used to guide them back?'

I could imagine them in my mind's eye, gaping holes in the body, wings and tail, creaking and swaying as the pilot sought to hold them steady for home, a wounded or dying crew, and the radio shot to bits. And I knew, from too recent experience, the bitter loneliness of the winter's sky at night, with no radio, no guide for home and the fog blotting out the land.

'That's right, sir. He used to go up for a second flight in the same night, patrolling out over the North Sea, looking for a crippled plane. Then he'd guide them home, back here to Minton, sometimes through fog so dense you couldn't see your hand. Sixth sense, they said he had; something of the Irish in him.'

I turned from the photograph and stubbed my cigarette butt into the ashtray by the bed. Joe was at the door.

'Quite a man,' I said, and I meant it. Even today, middle-aged, he was a superb flier.

'Oh yes, sir, quite a man, Mister Johnny. I

remember him saying to me once, standing right where you are before the fire: "Joe," he said, "whenever there's one of them out there in the night, trying to get back, I'll go out and bring him home."'

I nodded gravely. The old man so obviously worshipped his wartime officer.

'Well,' I said, 'by the look of it, he's still doing it.'

Now Joe smiled.

'Oh, I hardly think so, sir. Mister Johnny went out on his last patrol Christmas Eve 1943, just fourteen years ago tonight. He never came back, sir. He went down with his plane somewhere out there in the North Sea. Good night, sir. And Happy Christmas.'